Join the Cutiecorns on every adventure!

Heart of Gold

Purrfect Pranksters

Rainy Day Rescue

Carnival Chaos

Lost and Found

Cutiecorns

Lost and Found

by Shannon Penney

SCHOLASTIC INC.

Text copyright © 2022 by Shannon Decker
Illustrations copyright © 2022 by Scholastic Inc.

All rights reserved. Published by Scholastic Inc., *Publishers since 1920.* SCHOLASTIC and associated logos are trademarks and/or registered trademarks of Scholastic Inc.

The publisher does not have any control over and does not assume any responsibility for author or third-party websites or their content.

No part of this publication may be reproduced, stored in a retrieval system, or transmitted in any form or by any means, electronic, mechanical, photocopying, recording, or otherwise, without written permission of the publisher. For information regarding permission, write to Scholastic Inc., Attention: Permissions Department, 557 Broadway, New York, NY 10012.

This book is a work of fiction. Names, characters, places, and incidents are either the product of the author's imagination or are used fictitiously, and any resemblance to actual persons, living or dead, business establishments, events, or locales is entirely coincidental.

ISBN 978-1-338-84708-6
10 9 8 7 6 5 4 3 2 1   22 23 24 25 26

Printed in the U.S.A. 40
First printing 2022

Book design by Omou Barry

Chapter 1

"Oof!" Flash yelped as the ball bounced off her snout.

Sparkle raced over to her friend. "Are you okay? I didn't mean to let go. I'm just no match for your shifting magic!"

"I'm fine," Flash said with a laugh, rubbing her nose. "It's not the first time Magic Tug-of-War has ended that way!"

Sparkle gave Flash a squeeze and breathed a sigh of relief. The first-year pups were practicing their shifting magic in Mr. Magictail's class at Cutiecorn Academy. After all, Sparkle and her friends weren't just regular pups—they were Cutiecorns! All the dogs on Puppypaw Island had colorful horns between their ears that gave them special magical powers.

As a special treat, Mr. Magictail had brought the class outside for a round of Magic Tug-of-War! The rules were simple: Each pair of pups would use their shifting magic to pull a small ball through the air toward them. No paws allowed! Flash, a Yorkshire Terrier with a shimmering purple horn, was especially good at shifting magic. Sparkle had put up a good fight, but she wasn't surprised that her feisty friend had gotten the ball in the end!

Mr. Magictail clapped his paws. "Okay, class! Furbulous job today. Your magic skills are really growing!" He collected the balls in a big mesh bag. "It's almost time to go home, but Mrs. Horne would like to meet with all first-year Cutiecorns in the courtyard. She has a special announcement!"

The air filled with excited barks and yips. Mrs. Horne was the head of Cutiecorn Academy. If she was making a special announcement, it must be something ter-ruff-ically exciting!

Glitter, a white Maltese with a pink horn, bounded over to Sparkle and Flash. "A special announcement? What do you think it could be?"

"It is getting near the end of the school year," Sparkle said thoughtfully as they walked inside to collect their things. "Maybe she's throwing us a barbecue to celebrate! Or an ice-cream party!" As if on cue, Sparkle's stomach gave a loud grumble. She giggled. "Or maybe I'm just hungry."

"Tug-of-War with Flash really took it out of you, huh?" her Beagle friend Twinkle teased. "I got paired up with her last time. It made me hungry enough to eat a whole bag of bones!"

Flash grabbed her backpack from her locker and zoomed off down the hall. "Last one to the courtyard is a dawdling dog!" she called over her shoulder.

Sparkle smiled as she collected her things. Her friends were all so different—and had different magical strengths, too! That was what made them a pawsome team. Sparkle couldn't imagine life on Puppypaw Island without her three best buddies.

Sparkle, Glitter, and Twinkle trotted down the hall, through a giant stone archway, and out into the sunny courtyard. They sat with the rest of their classmates under a flowering tree. Everyone was barking up a storm about the announcement, but when Mrs. Horne stepped outside and waved a friendly paw, they fell silent immediately.

"Hello, first-year pups!" Mrs. Horne smiled, and her turquoise horn glittered in the sunlight. She held a folded piece of paper in one paw, but Sparkle couldn't see what it said. "As you all know, I have a special announcement for you today."

Sparkle's stomach flip-flopped in anticipation. She couldn't wait much longer, fur real!

"Your teachers are all so pleased with your progress this year," Mrs. Horne said kindly. "You've been working hard! We feel it's important for you to learn about different kinds of magic—and different cultures, too."

Sparkle glanced down at her charm bracelet. A charm with two paw prints twinkled up at her, and she remembered receiving it after helping with the Cutiecorn Carnival. Cutiecorns of all kinds had come to visit Puppypaw Island—cats, birds, goats, bunnies, and even hedgehogs!—for a puptastic carnival and talent show. Sparkle had loved meeting the new animals!

Mrs. Horne went on, "I'm happy to announce that tomorrow, you'll be taking your first overnight field trip. We'll get on the ferry bright and early."

Sparkle could hardly believe her ears. Hot diggity dog! A field trip!

While the rest of their classmates whispered breathlessly, Glitter raised a polite paw. "Where are we going?"

Mrs. Horne unfolded the paper she held to reveal a big, beautiful map. All the pups leaned forward eagerly, trying to get a better look. What was this place?

Chapter 2

"I can't believe it! I just can't believe it!" Sparkle's little brother, Zippy, raced in circles around her bedroom after dinner. He was a blur of golden fur. "A field trip! To Hopalong Haven, home of the bunnies! A whole different island! This is the most pawsome thing to happen since . . . well, ever!"

Sparkle laughed. "Barking bulldogs, slow down!" she woofed. "You're making me dizzy." Sparkle had to admit, her snout was spinning for lots of reasons. There was so much to think about!

Zippy plopped down on Sparkle's floor, breathing hard. "Being a big pup is so cool.

You get to learn magic AND go on overseas adventures!" He groaned dramatically. "I'm stuck here doing all the same things I always do."

"Your turn will come soon enough, big guy," Sparkle's mom reassured him from her perch on the bed. "Besides, we still haven't decided for sure that Sparkle is going on the trip."

Sparkle's eyes widened. *Not go?* The afternoon had been such a whirlwind, she'd never even considered not being allowed to go on the field trip.

Her mom looked at her carefully. "I have to admit, I'm nervous about sending you on your first trip away from Puppypaw Island without me or Dad. You're still young, Sparkle!"

Before Sparkle could say anything, Zippy flopped over with a paw to his forehead. "Mom! You have to let her go, you just have to!"

There was a gentle knock on the door, and their dad peeked in. "Is someone's tail on fire in here?" he joked.

Zippy rolled his eyes. "No, but even if it was, that wouldn't be half as exciting as Sparkle's field trip! And now Mom says she might not be able to go!"

Their dad looked thoughtful. "This trip is a very big deal, it's true." He looked at Sparkle. "Mom and I want to see how you're feeling about it before we make a decision."

"I'm definitely a little nervous," Sparkle admitted quietly. Then she sat up straight and looked her mom in the eyes. "But I also know

I can do it. I'm a responsible pup, and I really, really want to go! Please?"

Her mom smiled. "Oh, I know you're responsible, sweetie. This is just new for us, too. You'll be so far away!" She looked at Sparkle's dad. "What do you think?"

He didn't say anything for a minute, and Sparkle held her breath. She hadn't realized just how much she wanted to go on the trip until this very moment! She would do anything to convince them.

"I think that Sparkle can handle it," her dad finally said. "And even though it makes us nervous, I think we have to let her give it a try."

"I think you're right," Sparkle's mom said. Her eyes were a little teary as Sparkle threw herself into her arms for a hug.

"Oh, thank you, thank you!" Sparkle cried. "I promise I'll be safe and careful and polite and on my barking best behavior!"

"Wahoooooo!" Zippy woofed. He took a deep breath and unleashed a stream of questions. "What do you think Hopalong Haven will be like? How long is the boat ride? What do bunnies do for fun? Are their magical powers different from ours?"

Sparkle had to admit, she had a lot of the same questions! She started to feel those familiar butterflies fluttering around in her belly. The trip was so soon, and there was a lot she didn't know!

Sparkle's dad laughed. "I've been to Hopalong Haven," he said. "But learning the answers to those questions is part of the fun of going somewhere new. You should find those things out for yourself!" He patted Sparkle's paw. "I'm sure you're going to have a magical time, Sparkle."

Sparkle felt a jolt of excitement. If her dad thought she'd have fun, she trusted him!

Zippy, meanwhile, had pulled piles of clothes out of Sparkle's closet and dresser. "Do you think you'll need a snowsuit? How about a bathing suit? Maybe a tennis racket?"

"Whoa, whoa, whoa, I think some pajamas and a sweatshirt will work out just fine," their dad said with a chuckle. "Unless the bunnies are expert skiers, in which case you'll definitely need some extra gear." He winked at Sparkle.

"Don't forget your toothbrush!" Sparkle's mom waved a paw as she and their dad left the room.

With Zippy's help, Sparkle's bag was packed in no time! She closed it up and set it gently near the foot of her bed.

"Sparkle? Are you still . . . nervous?" Zippy asked after a minute.

Sparkle nodded, playing with the golden heart locket around her neck. "A little bit," she admitted. "I've never gone to another island.

I've never even been on the ferry before! It's a big day." She thought for a moment. "But I met some bunnies at the Cutiecorn Carnival. Remember Fluff, the little gray bunny who did such ter-ruff-ic tap dancing in the talent show? She was really sweet."

Zippy threw his paws around his sister in a big hug. "You're going to have a puptastic time, I just know it." He yawned and trotted toward the door. "G'night, Sparkle. Sleep tight!"

"'Night, Zippy," Sparkle said.

She snuggled down under her covers and turned off the light. From her bed, she could watch the stars outside her window. They twinkled, and flashed, and glittered against the black sky . . . Wait a minute!

The shining stars had reminded Sparkle of her best friends—Twinkle, Flash, and Glitter! They'd be with her for this whole crazy adventure. The thought made her feel much, much better. She could always be brave with her friends by her side!

The butterflies in Sparkle's stomach settled down for the night. Before she knew it, her eyes fluttered closed and she drifted off into a peaceful sleep. Sparkle was ready for whatever adventures the next day would bring!

Chapter 3

"I'm so excited, I can hardly bark!" Flash cried, racing ahead of her friends.

Twinkle rolled her eyes and groaned dramatically. "It's hard to tell the difference between super-excited Flash and regular, everyday-excited Flash." Twinkle pretended to be grumpy, but really she had a heart of gold.

Glitter and Sparkle giggled. The four friends carried their backpacks, but today they weren't going to school. Instead, they were on their way to the docks. It was field trip day!

Her puppy pals chatted as they walked, but Sparkle had a hard time concentrating on what they were barking about. The butterflies in her belly were back! They had started up again when she'd hugged her parents goodbye and promised to be safe and careful. Now they seemed to be flapping up a storm as she got closer to the docks.

"Hurry up, slowpups!" Flash ran circles around them. Her backpack bounced wildly on her little back, but she didn't even seem to notice!

Twinkle pointed a paw. "The dock is right down there," she said to Flash. "Bet I can get there first!"

Without another word, Flash and Twinkle zipped down the road as fast as their paws would take them.

Sparkle watched them go, with a little smile on her snout. She could see the bright blue water shining up ahead. Normally, the sight filled her with happiness—but today, it just made her feel even more nervous!

"Is everything okay, Sparkle?" Glitter asked quietly. She was especially good at caring magic, so she could always tell how other pups were feeling. It was no use trying to keep secrets from Glitter!

"I'm just a bit nervous about our field trip," Sparkle admitted. She adjusted her backpack straps. "I can't wait to see Hopalong Haven and meet the bunnies, but it's a big change.

We'll be so far from home! What if something goes wrong? I promised my parents that everything would be fine."

Glitter was quiet for a moment. "I feel like that a little bit, too. But it makes me feel much better to know that we'll all be on this trip together!" She put a paw around Sparkle's shoulders. "Even if something goes wrong, we'll be there to help one another."

The knot in Sparkle's stomach loosened a little. Glitter always knew just the right thing to say!

"Thanks, Glitter. That does help," she said.

Glitter grabbed her paw and squeezed. "I'm so glad—because it looks like our adventure is about to begin!"

The pups had reached the docks! The ferry

bobbed in the water up ahead, and some of their classmates had already begun climbing aboard. Mrs. Horne, Mr. Magictail, and old Captain Saltypaws stood on deck, greeting everyone.

Sparkle took a deep breath. This was it!

"Ahoy, young sailors!" Captain Saltypaws barked out as they boarded the ferry, tipping his hat. "Are you ready for a tail-waggingly good adventure on the high seas?"

Sparkle and Glitter couldn't help giggling.

"Aye-aye!" Sparkle said, raising her arm in a salute.

Captain Saltypaws threw his snout back and laughed. "That's what we like to hear! Welcome aboard!"

Sparkle and Glitter climbed the stairs to find Flash and Twinkle on the upper deck of the ferry.

"Flying fur balls, look at the view!" Flash barked, gesturing out to sea. The sunlight sparkled on the water for as far as they could see!

"Which way is Hopalong Haven?" Twinkle wondered aloud.

Mrs. Horne walked up behind them. "It's off in that direction," she said, pointing. "The boat ride should take about two hours, but you'll be able to see Hopalong Haven long before we arrive."

Just then, a foghorn sounded, making all the pups jump!

Captain Saltypaws's voice came over the crackling loudspeaker. "It's time to leave port!"

Everyone howled with excitement as the ferry's engine roared to life and the boat slowly eased away from the dock. They were off!

The butterflies in Sparkle's stomach flapped to life again as she watched Puppypaw Island grow smaller and smaller behind them. She could see the playground, Icy Paws Ice Cream Shop, even her house way up on the hilltop. It all looked so far away!

"We'll be back in the shake of a tail," Glitter whispered so only Sparkle could hear.

"Gather around, students!" Mr. Magictail called from the front of the boat. The class of twelve pups all sat down on a long bench, wiggling and chatting. Sparkle couldn't help noticing that one of their classmates, Scooter, sat alone and silent at the far end of the bench.

Mr. Magictail clapped his paws for attention. "Mrs. Horne and I thought a magic lesson would be just the thing to keep you scallywags busy during our journey," he said with a wink.

"That's right," Mrs. Horne added. "And since we're traveling across the water today, we're going to use water in our lesson, too!"

Scooter turned a bit green at the mention of water.

Mrs. Horne held up a clear jar of water. "Today's magic will require some different skills that you haven't used before! This is just for fun, so try your best. Watch me carefully." She concentrated on the jar of water, and her turquoise horn began to shimmer with magic. Before long, the clear water had turned a beautiful emerald green! Bow wow!

Sparkle could hardly believe her eyes. She'd never made anything change color before!

Mrs. Horne gave them a brilliant smile. "Let's pair off, and I'll give each pair a jar to practice on. Mr. Magictail and I will come around to assist you!"

Glitter turned to Sparkle. "Want to partner up?"

Sparkle glanced over at Scooter, sitting quietly by himself. "You know, Scooter seems like he's having a ruff time. Do you mind if I ask him to be my partner?"

"Of course not!" Glitter gave Sparkle a hug. "Your caring magic is growing by the day, you know. I think you're right—Scooter could really use your help!"

Sparkle walked slowly over to Scooter. The ferry bobbed and swayed a bit under her paws. "Hey, Scooter, can we be partners?"

Scooter gave her a weak smile. "Sure. But I'm not so sure how good my magic will be today."

"Is everything okay?" Sparkle asked, sitting down next to him.

Scooter hung his snout and peered down at his paws. "I'm a little scared of the water," he whispered. "I've never been on a boat before! My stomach feels all queasy."

Sparkle lowered her voice, too. "I totally understand. I'm so nervous about this trip!"

"You are?" Scooter's eyes widened. "You don't seem nervous!"

"I've been trying to hide it, just like you," Sparkle said. "But your secret is safe with me. And if you're feeling queasy, try this: Look straight ahead at the horizon where the sea meets the sky. Flash's dad taught me that the first time he took me out on his sailboat. He's an explorer!"

Scooter peered out at the horizon, and his shoulders relaxed a little. "That really helps. Thanks, Sparkle!"

"A jar for you two," Mrs. Horne said then, walking up and handing a jar of water to Sparkle.

"Are you ready to try some magic?" Sparkle asked.

"You bet your bulldogs I am!" Scooter said with a grin.

It took a few attempts, but eventually both pups managed to change the color of the water in their jar. Scooter turned it a deep, dark purple; then Sparkle changed it to a shimmering pink! All around them, their classmates were yipping and yapping with excitement. Flash had managed to turn the water in her jar a whole rainbow of colors all at once!

HONK!

The foghorn sounded again, causing all the pups to nearly jump out of their fur.

Captain Saltypaws's voice rang out over the loudspeaker. "Land ho!"

Sparkle leaped to her paws. Sure enough, in the distance, she could just see the outline of a lush, green island: Hopalong Haven!

Chapter 4

All twelve pups dashed over to the ferry railing for a better look—even Scooter! Happy woofs filled the air.

"It's so green!"

"It's bigger than I expected!"

"Those big peaks over there almost look like bunny ears!"

"I can see the dock!"

Sure enough, as the ferry drew closer to the island, the dock came into view. Just beyond it, Sparkle spotted a group of fuzzy creatures waving their paws in greeting—the bunnies! They wore warm smiles on their faces and hopped up and down in excitement.

Sparkle and her friends had met some bunnies at the Cutiecorn Carnival, but they were all different ages, and they hadn't gotten to talk to them much. She suddenly couldn't wait to spend the whole day with a group of bunnies her age. Just think of all the things she could learn from them! Her head swam with questions. The ferry couldn't dock soon enough!

The foghorn sounded again as the ferry came to a stop. The pups all jumped at the sound and giggled when they noticed the bunnies do the same on shore.

"We have reached the port, pups!" Captain Saltypaws announced. "Please take all your belongings and go ashore. Have a ter-ruff-ic visit—I'll see you tomorrow for your return journey!"

Sparkle and her classmates grabbed their backpacks and filed off the ferry slowly and shyly, behind Mrs. Horne and Mr. Magictail.

"Hello there!" A big, black bunny with a golden horn greeted them, twitching her nose. "I'm Mrs. McBun, and this is my class of first-year students. Welcome to Hopalong Haven!"

Behind her, the group of a dozen bunnies waved wildly, bouncing on their paws and calling out "Hi" and "Welcome!" They came in all colors and sizes. Some had tall ears, others had floppy ears, but between all their ears was a shimmering, colorful horn. Just like the Cutiecorn pups, the Cutiecorn bunnies had horns—and magical powers!

Sparkle's eyes lit up as she recognized Fluff, the little gray bunny they'd met at the carnival. Fluff looked like she was having a hard time not hopping over and hugging her puppy pals!

"We're so doggone happy to be here," Mrs. Horne said. "Thank you for inviting us. This is an exciting day for our group of pups!"

"Bow wow, it sure is!" Flash cried, unable to contain herself. The pups and bunnies all giggled.

"We figured you'd be hungry after your journey," Mrs. McBun went on, "and I know you packed lunches. Should we start our visit with a picnic?"

The pups and bunnies all cheered and fell in step behind Mrs. McBun, Mrs. Horne, and Mr. Magictail.

"Hi!" cried Fluff, hopping over to Sparkle, Glitter, Flash, and Twinkle. "I'm so glad you're here!" She threw her paws around Twinkle first, then the others in turn. Her fur tickled Sparkle's nose, and Sparkle couldn't help laughing.

"We're so glad to see you!" Twinkle replied. "We can't wait to explore your island and meet your friends."

"Oh, let me introduce you to some of them! You made me feel so at home on Puppypaw Island. I want to do the same for all of you!" Fluff said, turning to the bunnies hopping beside her. "This is Beans, Flops, and Scamper." Then she looked at the group ahead of them and pointed a paw. One speck-led bunny up front was flipping in the air with every other step! "That up there is Twitch. He keeps us all on our toes!"

Sparkle watched Twitch bound ahead with fascination. He was like the bunny version of Flash!

In no time at all, their path opened up

into a small, grassy field on the water's edge. Sparkle could see the glimmering blue water stretch out to the horizon. Low, fuzzy green plants that Sparkle didn't recognize grew all around the edge of the field.

"Welcome to Carrot Cove!" Mrs. McBun said, holding her arms wide. "This is the bunnies' favorite picnic spot. Settle in, get to know one another a bit, and enjoy your lunch!"

Sparkle, Glitter, Twinkle, and Flash followed Fluff to a grassy spot with the rest of the Cutiecorns. They pulled out their lunchboxes. Holy bones, Sparkle was hungry!

"What are those plants around the edge of the field?" Glitter asked, taking a bite of her peanut butter and jelly sandwich. "I've never seen those before."

Fluff's face stretched into a wide smile. "They're carrots! Rows and rows of carrots, as far as the eye can see! That's how Carrot Cove got its name."

Sparkle could hardly believe her ears. Those didn't look like the carrots she was used to! The carrots she usually ate were orange and crunchy, not green and leafy.

Beans the bunny noticed her confusion. "Carrots grow under the ground," he explained. "The green part you see is just the top! If you tug on one, you'll unearth a carrot. Go on, try it!"

Sparkle's eyes grew wide. She reached a paw over and pulled on one of the green plants. She felt it give way. Sure enough, a bright orange carrot appeared on the end!

"Hot diggity dog!" Flash cried. "I had no idea that's how carrots grow!"

"Me neither," admitted Sparkle, tucking the carrot into her backpack. "That was so cool!"

As lunch went on, the pups and bunnies chatted happily, telling stories about life on their different islands. Twitch, the speckled bunny, kept everyone laughing with his mid-meal dance break. He busted out some crazy moves and got everyone else to join in. (Flash even taught him some new moves of her own!) "Dancing is good for your digestion," Twitch explained with a silly grin.

Sparkle hadn't laughed so hard in a long time. What had she been so worried about? Their first day on Hopalong Haven was off to a puptastic start!

Chapter 5

Mrs. McBun clapped her paws for attention. "If everyone is done eating, we'd love to give you a tour of our island!"

The pups all cheered. They couldn't wait to see more of Hopalong Haven! If Carrot Cove was any indication, this place would be full of surprises.

Everyone packed up their lunches and headed across the field. At the far end, they followed a wide path into a bright green forest. Colorful flowers covered the ground and wound up the tree trunks on thick vines. It was like nothing Sparkle had ever seen before . . . and it smelled amazing!

"Wow," she breathed. "Our forests on Puppypaw Island have a lot of pine trees. This forest is so vivid and bright!"

Scamper the bunny plucked two big, purple flowers from alongside the path. She tucked one behind her floppy ear and handed the other to Sparkle. "Aren't they pretty? The best part is that all the flowers on Hopalong Haven are edible, too!"

Sparkle wrinkled her snout in confusion and looked down at the flower in her paw. Was she supposed to eat it?

Scamper laughed. "We don't usually nibble flowers fresh out of the ground—though they're delicious however you eat them! We add them to our meals in different ways. You'll see at dinner tonight."

"Bow wow, did you hear that?" Sparkle asked, turning to Twinkle. "They add flowers to their cooking!"

Twinkle made a face and stuck out her tongue. "I'm not so sure about eating them," she said, taking the purple flower from Sparkle's paw and tucking it behind her golden ear, "but they look great as accessories!"

Before long, Sparkle noticed that the forest path had started to slope upward. They were walking uphill now, but she had been so busy looking around and talking to the bunnies that she had hardly even realized it! The sun shone through the leafy branches above them, warming her fur. This was turning out to be a totally ter-ruff-ic day!

The path led them to a lush, grassy meadow, much bigger than Carrot Cove. The bunnies broke into a run, hopping and bouncing and cartwheeling across the open grass. The pups couldn't help joining in, too!

Flops, the brown-and-white bunny Fluff had introduced them to earlier, pointed a paw at the far end of the meadow. "That's Lettuce Lea, my favorite place on the whole island. You're going to love it!"

As they got closer and closer, Sparkle could see why Lettuce Lea was a popular spot. It was a playground and adventure park! There were huge hollow tree stumps to run over, under, and even through. Little waterfalls tumbled onto flat stones, making perfect places to splash and cool off. Swinging ropes hung from the trees!

"This place is incrediwoof!" Flash barked, racing straight for one of the waterfalls. She skidded through the water and then shook off her fur. "Refreshing!"

Sparkle ran to join her friend, with the rest of the Cutiecorns close behind. She noticed that Scooter, who she'd sat with on the ferry, steered clear of the waterfalls but bounded off to try one of the rope swings. She was glad that he seemed to be having so much fun after a ruff start!

A little later, Sparkle spotted Flash and Twitch standing at either end of a long, hollowed-out log. "On your mark, get set, go!" Flash cried.

Neither one of them moved. What was going on?

Then Sparkle noticed Flash's purple horn glowing brighter and brighter. Twitch's royal blue horn did the same! Grins stretched across both their faces as they stood in place, concentrating hard.

"They're playing tug-of-war with their shifting magic!" Glitter said quietly, walking up next to Sparkle.

Sure enough, after a few minutes, a small, shiny stone came out of Flash's end of the hollow log! Flash reached up and caught it with her paw. She was the winner!

Twitch flopped onto his back dramatically, with one paw to his forehead. "Your shifting magic is crazy good," he said. Then he leaped to his paws. "I demand a rematch!"

Sparkle and the rest of the onlookers all laughed. She had a feeling that Flash and Twitch could do this for hours!

All around the adventure park, pups and bunnies began practicing their magic skills. Mrs. Horne, Mr. Magictail, and Mrs. McBun cheered them on, offering tips and tricks.

Sparkle impressed some bunnies by navigating part of the park's obstacle course with her eyes closed, using just her feeling magic. Twitch tried it, too, and she couldn't believe how fast he moved. Twitch's feeling magic was barking good!

"High paw!" he cried, joining Sparkle at the end of the course and tapping her paw with his.

Together, they watched as Twinkle used her amazing seeing magic to win a game of magical hide-and-seek. Some of the other Cutiecorns played tag, their horns shimmering as they used their magic to their advantage. Off to one side, Fluff showed off her tap-dancing skills on top of a tree stump—no magic required!

Sparkle couldn't help thinking about how different the pups and bunnies were. Their islands were different, they ate different foods, and they even used their magic differently sometimes! But they also had a lot more in common than she'd expected. She was learning so much from the bunnies already . . . and their adventure had only just begun!

Chapter 6

The afternoon at the adventure park flew by in the twitch of a tail! Before Sparkle knew it, the sun was dipping lower in the sky. Her stomach let out a loud grumble.

"Uh-oh. Was that thunder rolling in or just your stomach?" Twinkle joked.

"Did someone say 'stomach?'" Flash asked,

dashing over to her friends. "My stomach is barking at me like crazy. 'Feeeeed me, Flash! Feed me!'"

Sparkle laughed. "For some reason, that doesn't surprise me at all." Flash had a reputation for being a bottomless pit! She needed a lot of food to keep up her pawsome energy.

A loud whistle came from one end of Lettuce Lea, where Mrs. McBun waved a paw in the air. "Gather around, Cutiecorns!"

The pups and bunnies all raced over to join the grown-ups. Sparkle couldn't wait to hear what they were doing next.

"I hope you've all worked up a big appetite because our next stop is dinner!" Mrs. McBun announced.

The Cutiecorns cheered loudly. Flash and Twitch both did excited backflips and gave each other a high five.

"Dinner tonight will be at Treetop Towers," Mrs. McBun explained, once the cheers quieted down. "This is another one of our favorite spots in all of Hopalong Haven, so you pups are in for a treat. Follow me!"

Chatting and barking happily, the pups and bunnies fell into a loose line behind the grown-ups. The sky was turning pink, yellow, and orange as they headed across the field and onto a different wooded path. This path was dotted with light posts, but the woods glowed in the sunset. Sparkle felt warm and happy, surrounded by friends new and old. This had been a day she would remember furever!

"Ooh, what's that?" Glitter asked a few minutes later, pointing up ahead.

A bright golden glow shone through the trees. Sparkle tried to make out what it was. As they walked closer, her breath caught in her throat.

"Oh, it's beautiful!" she said with a sigh.

They had arrived at Treetop Towers! The clearing before them was strung with twinkling lights. Wooden ramps and tunnels led up into the trees in all different directions. As the pups tipped their snouts back to look up, they could see platforms, tree houses, tunnels, and bridges crisscrossing overhead. It was a magical sight! Beautiful music drifted through the air, and Sparkle closed her eyes for a minute to listen. They had nothing like this back on Puppypaw Island!

After a silent moment of awe, the pups all began barking at once.

"Bow WOW, this is amazing!"

"I've never been up in the trees before!"

"Look at all the different paths!"

Sparkle took a quick glance over at Scooter. He'd been scared on the ferry earlier. Would he be okay with a treetop dinner? Luckily, Scooter was woofing with excitement, just like the other pups. Sparkle smiled and gave him a little wave.

"Scamper, would you like to lead us to

dinner?" Mrs. McBun asked the little orange bunny standing near the front of the group.

"Sure!" Scamper said shyly. "My dad is a chef at Treetop Towers, so I spend a lot of time here."

A chef? Pawsome! Sparkle had never known a real chef before. She had so many questions!

She bounded over to Scamper as the little bunny headed to the ramp, and they fell into step together. "Do you ever help your dad cook? What kinds of things do you like to make?"

Scamper nodded eagerly. "Oh, yes—I love to help in the kitchen! My favorite thing to make is breakfast. Carrot pancakes with real maple syrup are my specialty!"

Sparkle's eyes widened. "You eat pancakes, too? I've only ever had my mom's pancakes, but I'd love to try yours one day. I've never made them myself before!"

"It's not too hard," Scamper said. "I can give you my special recipe to try when you get home, if you want."

Sparkle clapped her paws. "I'd love that!"

Sparkle and Scamper chatted happily as they led the group higher and higher into the trees. The ramp they were walking along suddenly turned into a tunnel. Barking bulldogs, Sparkle had never been in a tunnel like this before! It was lined with little lights, but it still felt dark. She wasn't so sure she liked it! Luckily, she could see the end of the tunnel up ahead. She took a deep breath.

Scamper noticed her hesitation. "Not too much farther!" she said encouragingly.

As they continued on, Sparkle marveled at how well Scamper knew her way around this place. There were so many different ways to go, but the little orange bunny never hesitated.

"Just follow your nose!" Scamper said with a wink.

Sure enough, when Sparkle sniffed the air, she could smell the most amazing things. Whatever was cooking in the treetops was going to be a puptastic treat!

After a few minutes, they paused on a platform to let the rest of the group catch up. Sparkle spotted Flash and Twitch bounding up the ramp together. Twinkle walked with Scooter and Fluff, deep in conversation about something. The rest of the pups and bunnies all filed in, sniffing the air and commenting on the delicious smells.

But . . . where was Glitter?

Sparkle's eyes darted back and forth over all the Cutiecorns on the platform. The white Maltese was nowhere to be seen! Sparkle felt her stomach begin to churn, and not because she was hungry. Where was her friend?

Bow wow—Glitter was missing!

Chapter 7

Sparkle felt her golden horn begin to tingle. She had to find Glitter—and fast!

"I'll be right back," she whispered to Scamper. Before the bunny could ask any questions, she quietly slipped to the back of the group and headed down the ramp.

Sparkle paused for a moment, wondering if she should ask the teachers for help. What if Glitter was in real trouble? What if Sparkle got lost, too? But Sparkle also didn't want to embarrass her friend. Glitter had probably just lost her way! Sparkle thought about how she would feel if a whole search party came looking for her when she had taken a wrong turn. Barking bulldogs, how humiliating!

No, Sparkle would look for Glitter herself— she trusted her magic! But if she couldn't find her quickly, she'd return to the teachers for help. She had promised her parents that she'd be responsible, and now she had to prove it!

Sparkle glanced over her shoulder. Whew! No one had noticed her slip away. She raced quickly down the ramp. Her golden horn was glowing brightly in the darkness now! When she reached the first intersection, Sparkle stood very still and listened to her magic. She turned right, through a long, twisty tunnel. She was sure they hadn't come up this way!

Just when it felt like Sparkle would never reach the end of the tunnel, she saw the round exit up ahead. And there, standing nervously on a platform all alone, was Glitter.

"Bow wow, am I glad to see you!" Sparkle barked.

"Sparkle!" Glitter threw her paws around her friend's neck. "I must have taken a wrong turn. I was so busy looking at the stars and the twinkling lights that I got separated from the group." She hung her snout. "I'm so embarrassed!"

Sparkle gave her a squeeze. "Don't be! There's a lot to see here, and it's easy to get overwhelmed. Plus, if we're quick, no one will even know we were missing. Pup's honor!"

Together, the two friends dashed back up through the tunnel. "How did you find me, anyway?" Glitter panted.

Sparkle shrugged. "Actually, I used my magic! It told me right where you were."

"Your feeling magic is getting so strong, Sparkle," Glitter said with a sweet smile. "I'm proud of you—and thankful!"

The two pups emerged from the tunnel, turned left up the ramp, and caught sight of their group ahead. Some of them had begun climbing a ladder to the restaurant, paw over paw, while the others waited their turn.

Sparkle and Glitter exchanged relieved glances and quietly joined the back of the line. They'd made it, and no one had noticed that they were gone!

When it was her turn to climb the ladder, Sparkle moved quickly. Her paws were steady . . . until her snout popped up over the top. She was so surprised at what she saw that she almost lost her grip!

Treetop Towers's restaurant stretched out before her, a huge tree house filled with long tables, a dance floor, and even a stage! A bunny band played lively music, and webs of colorful lights hung all around. Sparkle had seen a lot of furbulous things today, but this was the best, paws down. It was truly magical!

When Glitter reached the tree house, the two friends joined the rest of their group at a long wooden table. There were big platters of food almost as far as the eye could see! Even though Sparkle didn't recognize a lot of the dishes, she couldn't wait to dig in!

A big white bunny wearing a chef's hat perched behind his silver horn hopped up to the end of their table. "Hello, Cutiecorns— and welcome, pups! We're so happy to have you at Treetop Towers." The pups and bunnies all clapped. *This must be Scamper's dad!* "Tonight, we're serving some of Hopalong Haven's most famous dishes, including a tasty veggie stir-fry with noodles; dandelion green pizza; festive fruit salad with mint; and, of course, carrot cake with cream cheese icing for dessert. Enjoy!" He gave them a deep bow and turned back toward the kitchen.

The Cutiecorns all began to fill their plates. Sparkle couldn't wait to try a little of everything! Scamper leaned over, pointing at the pizza on her plate. "See the little purple things scattered on top? Those are the flower petals I showed you earlier!"

Sparkle took a cautious bite. Yum! Her mouth popped with a bunch of delicious new flavors all at once. Bow wow, that was good!

The rest of the evening flew by in a whirl-wind of ter-ruff-ic food, upbeat music, and crazy dancing. Unsurprisingly, Twitch and Flash were the first ones out on the dance floor, leading the group in sillier and sillier moves until they were all bent over laughing! The bunnies had some fun, bouncy dance steps that Sparkle had never tried before. After a while, her paws were so tired she could barely stand!

A familiar voice crackled over the microphone. Mrs. McBun was up onstage! "All right, everyone! I don't know about you, but I think it's time to put my dancing shoes away for the night. Who's ready for a slumber party?"

Cheers rang in the air as the pups and bunnies collected their things. Sparkle was so doggone tired, she hardly noticed the climb down out of Treetop Towers. Before she knew it, they were back on the soft grass.

"Luckily, the burrows aren't far," Beans the bunny said, noticing that Sparkle's paws were dragging. "We'll be there in the twitch of a whisker!"

"Burrows?" Sparkle asked. She hadn't heard that word before!

Beans's eyes lit up. "Oh yes! The burrows are a series of underground tunnels where we sleep at night. They're super cozy!"

Sparkle felt a flutter of nerves in her belly again. Underground tunnels? She wasn't so sure she liked that idea.

Scooter, walking just in front of them, seemed thrilled. "That sounds pawsome!" he cried. "I bet the tunnels are nice and toasty. I can't wait for this slumber party!"

Sparkle shrugged.

"Hey, is everything okay?" Scooter asked

quietly, falling into step beside her. "Are you nervous about the burrows?"

"A little bit," Sparkle admitted. "I've never gone underground before."

Scooter smiled. "You helped me be brave on the boat this morning. Now it's my turn! I'll help you feel brave in the tunnels."

Sparkle felt better already. "Deal," she said with a grin.

Moments later, the group came to a halt in front of a round hole in the side of a little hill. It was surrounded by grass and ivy, and Sparkle could see little twinkle lights lining the tunnel inside.

"Welcome to the burrows!" Mrs. McBun announced. "We'll walk single file through the tunnels until we reach the den. It's big enough for all of us to sleep in comfortably. Follow me!"

Sparkle took a deep breath.

"You've got this," Scooter said. "I'm right behind you."

Sparkle could hear Flash up ahead in the tunnel already, barking up a storm. "This is the coolest! Maybe I can get my dad to build some tunnels like this at home. Did you use shovels? How many shovels do you have on Hopalong Haven? I can't imagine doing all this digging. My paws are tired just thinking about it!"

With a giggle, Sparkle stepped forward into the tunnel. This would be an adventure . . . right?

Chapter 8

The tunnels were brightly lit, and Sparkle felt herself relax as they wound deeper into the burrows. They passed through a few different intersecting paths, and Sparkle followed the group closely into each new tunnel.

Scooter chatted happily behind her. He was a good distraction! In front of her, Sparkle could see Glitter's pink horn glowing faintly.

She felt safe knowing that her friend's strong caring magic was at work!

After a few minutes, the tunnels opened up into a huge underground den. The whole room was carved out of dirt, but the floor was lined with soft, fuzzy carpet. Off to one side, sleeping bags and pillows were arranged in a big circle. Hundreds of lanterns hung from the ceiling, giving the room a warm glow.

"Ooh, this is so cozy!" Glitter whispered, giving Sparkle's paw a squeeze.

The pups and bunnies clambered to choose their sleeping bags, eager to snuggle in and get comfortable. Sparkle found a purple sleeping bag between Glitter and Twitch. Her paws were pounding from all the walking they had done. It felt grrrrrreat to lie down!

Once the Cutiecorns were all settled, Mrs. McBun had one last surprise for them. She gestured to a brown-speckled adult bunny with a bronze horn who had entered the den. "Friends, this is Mr. Hiphop. He is Hopalong Haven's best and funniest storyteller. He's here to tell you a bedtime story!"

The bunnies all clapped wildly, and the pups looked around, curious. Mr. Hiphop was awfully popular! As they snuggled down in their sleeping bags, they soon found out why. He told them a bunny pirate tale filled with action, adventure—and lots of laughs! Sparkle giggled so hard that she could barely catch her breath. Across the circle, Flash was laughing so much she couldn't bark a single word— which was unusual for her!

When the story was over, the group gave Mr. Hiphop a giant round of applause. Mrs. McBun, Mrs. Horne, and Mr. Magictail made sure that everyone was settled in before dimming the lanterns and climbing into their own sleeping bags for the night.

"Sweet dreams, Cutiecorns!" Mrs. Horne said as the den grew silent.

Sparkle shifted in her sleeping bag, listening to the deep breathing of everyone around her. Glitter had drifted off to sleep almost instantly. Twitch wiggled around for a few minutes, then began to snore softly. Sparkle stared up at the dim lanterns for what felt like hours. She was doggone tired, but she felt shaky and weak. She began to breathe faster. Now that she was alone with her thoughts in the dark, she knew one thing for sure—she didn't like being underground at all. She started to panic. Sparkle needed some fresh air . . . and fast!

Quietly, she climbed to her paws and tip-toed back toward the tunnel. Luckily, it was still lit with twinkle lights. Sparkle trotted down the tunnel, feeling her heart pounding in her chest. She felt so closed in! She needed to see the big, wide-open sky again.

Before long, she came to an intersection. Oh no! Sparkle couldn't remember which way led outside. Was it left? Or right? She thought for a minute, then turned left and began to run as fast as her paws would take her. Up ahead was another intersection. Was this the way? Should she turn around and go back? She decided to turn left again, and continued along to the next intersection.

There, Sparkle spun around, confused. She wasn't even sure which tunnel she had just come from. Barking bulldogs, what a mess!

She was hopelessly lost . . . and completely alone.

Panic rose in her throat, and her eyes filled with tears. This had been a terrible mistake! She should have stayed in her sleeping bag. Now she was all by herself, in the middle of the night, with no idea where to go or what to do next. Maybe her mom had been right to

want her to stay home. Now she'd definitely never be allowed to go on another field trip . . . if she ever made it out of these tunnels! Her paws trembled and her heart thudded.

Sparkle wrapped a paw around her golden heart-shaped locket. It had belonged to her mom, and to Grandma Shimmer before that. "Help," she whispered, squeezing her eyes shut tight. "What do I do now?"

Chapter 9

Suddenly, Sparkle felt her golden horn begin to tingle slightly. Of course! Her feeling magic! The answer had been with her all along. If she could calm down and focus, she could use her magic to lead her out of the tunnels, just like she had used it to help Glitter at Treetop Towers!

Sparkle took a deep breath, trying to calm her nerves. She felt her horn begin to glow brighter and brighter, and warm magic surged through her. Without hesitating, she began to follow where the magic guided her—right at the next intersection, left at the one after that, twisting through one dimly lit tunnel after another.

The air shifted around her, suddenly cooler and crisper. The exit was just up ahead! She raced down the last tunnel, then tumbled out into the fresh night air. The stars twinkled above her, and a cool breeze made the leaves dance.

Holy bones, she had made it!

Panting, Sparkle plopped down in the soft grass. She needed to rest her tired paws for a minute!

She took some deep breaths. It felt grrrreat to be back aboveground! Her heart stopped pounding, and she felt the breeze ruffle her fur.

Now what?

Sparkle hadn't thought about what to do next. She didn't want to go back into the burrow, but she also didn't want to be outside all alone. Hopalong Haven was puptastic, but it was still strange and new to her. It didn't seem safe to spend the night in the woods by—

A faint noise reached her ears. What was that? There it was again . . . and this time it sounded like it was getting closer.

Sparkle darted behind a tree. Was something after her? Her tail trembled and her fur stood on end. She had barely caught her breath, and now she was in danger all over again!

The noise moved closer and closer. It sounded like pawsteps! Was it coming from the tunnels? Sparkle squeezed her eyes shut. Maybe if she couldn't see whatever it was, it wouldn't be able to see her, either.

"Sparkle?"

Sparkle's eyes flew open. Peeking around the tree trunk was a familiar speckled face with a royal blue horn glowing in the starlight.

"Twitch?" Sparkle stared in surprise. "What are you doing out here?"

Twitch gave a little shrug. "My magic woke me up. I have strong feeling magic—just like you! I noticed that your sleeping bag was empty, and I had the feeling that something was wrong. My magic brought me out here, to you."

Sparkle blinked. It was strange to see energetic Twitch acting so calm and quiet!

"I have to really concentrate on my feeling magic," Twitch explained. It was like he knew what she was thinking! "It's not as strong when I'm acting all silly and crazy."

"Well, hot dog, I'm so grateful that you're here," Sparkle said with a smile. "Thank you for coming to look for me!"

Twitch tilted his head. "What are you doing all the way out here, anyway?"

Sparkle couldn't help feeling embarrassed. "I was having trouble falling asleep in the burrow," she said with a sigh. "I've never been underground before, and it makes me nervous. You've all been so wonderful and welcoming, and I don't want to seem ungrateful! I'm just not used to being closed in like that."

"That makes sense," Twitch said softly. "I'm sure there are lots of things on Puppypaw Island that would feel strange to me, too. I've never left Hopalong Haven before. I think you pups are really brave for coming here!"

A warm feeling filled Sparkle's belly. She was so glad she had told Twitch how she was feeling!

"But I'm not sure what to do now," Sparkle admitted with a yawn. "I'm really tired, but I don't think I'm ready to go back into the burrow." She glanced over at the dark tunnel and felt a shiver run through her fur.

Twitch looked thoughtful for a minute. "I have a hopping good idea!"

Before Sparkle could lift a paw, Twitch was bouncing around the clearing with the energy of a dozen bunnies. Flying fur balls, he moved fast!

A moment later, Twitch threw his paws in the air. "Ta-da! We'll camp out under the stars!"

Sparkle could see that he had created a cozy little sleeping spot right next to one of the colorful flowering shrubs. The ground there was mossy and soft, and Twitch had lined it with extra grass clippings.

"It's pawfect!" she exclaimed, giving her friend a hug. "Thank you so much for understanding, and for helping me."

"That's what friends are for," Twitch said, bounding into the sleeping spot and snuggling down.

Sparkle joined him, feeling warm and safe.

She peered up at the stars. They twinkled in the dark night sky, reminding her of the stars she had looked at the night before through her bedroom window. These were the same stars she could see on Puppypaw Island! Maybe her mom and dad were looking up at them even now.

The thought of it covered Sparkle like a toasty blanket, and she drifted off into a sweet, dreamless sleep.

Chapter 10

Sparkle woke to the feeling of the warm sun on her fur. She rolled over, stretched, and opened her eyes. The bright green leaves and blue sky overhead reminded her—she was on Hopalong Haven, and it was morning!

"Morning, sleepyfur!" Twitch said with a wave. He was sitting on a nearby tree stump, nibbling some kind of pastry. "I went into the burrow this morning to let everyone know where we were. I didn't want them to worry! I grabbed some breakfast, in case you were hungry." He held out a plate filled with yummy-looking breakfast treats. "The carrot croissants are my personal favorite, but you really can't go wrong with any of these."

Sparkle stood up, shaking out her arms and legs. She'd slept doggone hard!

"Thank you so much for taking care of everything," she said, grabbing a croissant and taking a bite. Bow wow, that was good!

Twitch gave an exaggerated bow. "Happy to help!"

Sparkle giggled. Suddenly, she could hear pawsteps in the distance. They moved closer

and closer. This time, she knew exactly where they were coming from!

"Good moooorning!" barked Flash, running out of the tunnels and then clapping a paw over her eyes. "Flying fur balls, it's bright out here!"

The whole group of pups and bunnies emerged after her, chatting and laughing. Some called out hello to Sparkle and Twitch, some waved, but no one made a big deal out of the fact that Sparkle had left the burrow. Thank goodness!

Glitter walked over and gave her a hug. "Everything okay?" she asked quietly.

Sparkle smiled and nodded. "I'm totally puptastic! Thanks."

Mrs. Horne placed a paw on Sparkle's shoulder. "I'm glad to hear it," she said, her eyes twinkling. "New things can be scary sometimes, but I'm proud of you for figuring out a safe solution that helped you feel comfortable. I'm sure your parents will be very proud, too."

"Bellies full?" Mrs. McBun asked the group. "Paws rested?" The pups and bunnies all nodded. "Then it's time to head to the docks!"

The whole group let out a loud groan.

Mrs. McBun laughed. "I'm glad that you've all had such a furbulous visit! Don't worry, we'll do it again soon."

With that, the group hopped and trotted out of the woods, down the path to the water's edge. Sparkle thought the water was a more brilliant blue today than she'd ever seen! It was calm, flat, and glinted like diamonds in the morning sunlight.

As they approached the docks, a familiar foghorn sounded. Everyone jumped out of their fur—even Mrs. Horne! Then they all dissolved into giggles. Captain Saltypaws waved to them from the deck of the ferry, a big smile on his gruff old snout.

"We want to thank the bunnies of Hopalong Haven for such a magical visit,"

Mrs. Horne announced, once the laughter had died down. "And even though we have to go, this isn't goodbye, it's 'see you later!'"

The pups and bunnies all exchanged happy hugs. Twitch gave Sparkle a big squeeze. "If I come visit Puppypaw Island, will you help me be brave? I'm not used to chewing on dog bones all day or running after tennis balls for hours on end." He winked.

Sparkle burst out laughing. "That's not what we do there!" she woofed. "But yes, come visit and I'll give you a top-dog tour."

Twitch did a backflip. "It's a deal!"

The pups waved to their new friends as they followed Mrs. Horne and Mr. Magictail onto the ferry.

"Welcome aboard, pups!" Captain Saltypaws

greeted them. "Ready to face down the roiling seas?"

Sparkle and her friends all stared at him.

"I think he just means 'Ready to set sail?'" Twinkle said, rolling her eyes.

"Ohhh!" Flash said. "Then aye-aye, Captain!"

Captain Saltypaws saluted them and headed for the wheelhouse while they all climbed to the upper deck.

As the ferry pulled away from the dock, the pups waved their paws as hard as they could at their new friends. The bunnies waved back, calling out farewells.

"We'll miss you!"

"Come back soon!"

"Don't forget, a carrot a day keeps the doctor away!"

(That last one was Twitch, of course.)

As Hopalong Haven faded into the distance, Mrs. Horne asked the pups to gather around. "We've had quite the adventure," she said, smiling at each of them in turn. "I'm very proud of all of you. You were kind, you were brave, and you were all open to trying new things. Going to a new place for the first time can be scary. Thank you for being such wonderful ambassadors for Puppypaw Island!"

Glitter squeezed Sparkle's shoulder, and Twinkle gave her a wink.

"I think you've all certainly earned these," Mrs. Horne went on, opening her paw. She held a bunch of beautiful golden charms . . . in the shape of little carrots! "You can add

these to your charm bracelets. This way, you'll always remember our friends on Hopalong Haven and what you learned there."

The pups all had wide grins on their snouts as Mrs. Horne attached a charm to each of their bracelets. Sparkle admired hers, shining in the morning sunlight. This one would always be extra special to her!

The rest of the ferry ride seemed to go by in the twitch of a tail. They sang songs, practiced magic lessons, and told stories about their favorite parts of Hopalong Haven. Before long, a bark rang through the air.

"Land ho!" Flash woofed, pointing out in front of the ferry.

Sure enough, a familiar paw-shaped island had just come into view on the horizon. A warm feeling filled Sparkle from her ears to her tail. Puppypaw Island!

Twinkle stepped up next to Sparkle and leaned on the ferry railing. "That was a ter-ruff-ic adventure, but it's good to be home, isn't it?"

Sparkle put a paw around her friend's shoulders. "You bet your bark it is!"

About the Author

Shannon Penney doesn't have any magical powers, but she has ter-ruff-ic fun writing about them! If she were a Cutiecorn, she'd have a turquoise horn and the ability to turn everything to ice cream. For now, she'll settle for the ice and snow of New Hampshire, where she writes, edits, and goes on adventures with her husband, two kids, and their non-magical cat.

DON'T MISS THE CUTIECORNS' NEXT
ADVENTURE: SCHOOL SPIRIT

Chapter 1

"Ohhh, it smells furbulous in here!" Flash cried. She pretended to melt into a puddle on the floor of the Pawfect Slice pizza parlor.

Her Beagle friend, Twinkle, rolled her eyes. "What a surprise, Flash is hungry," she joked.

Flash leaped to her paws and raced to the counter. Her tongue lolled out of her mouth as she peered at all the different pizza slices.

"What'll it be today, pups?" Bruno, the Bulldog owner of the Pawfect Slice, grinned at Flash and her friends. They visited regularly, and Bruno was always doggone happy to see them.

Flash scratched her head. "Can I have one of everything?"

Bruno chuckled. "You've always been a little pup with a huge appetite, but that might be too much even for you!"

Flash, Twinkle, Glitter, and Sparkle all ordered and paid for their slices—just one for each of them!—then plopped down in a nearby booth.

"Holy bones, I'm so excited for tomorrow!" Glitter, a white Maltese, said, waving a paw over her slice to cool it off.

"My big brother, Dash, says that Spirit

Week is one of the biggest weeks of the year at Cutiecorn Academy," Flash said around a mouthful of pizza. "It's going to be grrrreat!"

Flash and her friends were first-year students at Cutiecorn Academy. They weren't just regular pups—they were Cutiecorns! All the pups on Puppypaw Island had colorful horns between their ears that gave them special magical powers. The first-year pups were just learning to use their magic. Since they were new to Cutiecorn Academy, they were learning all the school's traditions for the first time, too!

Sparkle the Golden Retriever grinned, and her golden horn shimmered in the lights of the pizza parlor. "What do you think Spirit Week will be like?"